SPACE WITCH

To
Tino and Patricia
Carey and Candace
Danny and Penny

SPACE WITCH

WITCH

DON FREEMAN

NEW YORK 11364 **THE VIKING PRESS**

Late one autumn afternoon Tilly Ipswitch, Queen of Halloween, came flying home on her broomstick, carrying a book called *What Every Space Traveler Ought to Know.* She had bought it at the planetarium, where she had been studying the stars.

5

Tilly landed on her craggy mountain peak, parked her broom in the broomport, and scurried into her rickety old house. Her pet cat, Kit, was there at the top of the stairs, purring a warm welcome.

While Kit had his supper Tilly began to read all about space ships and satellites. Finally she said, "Kit, how would you like to spend Halloween frightening creatures on other planets?"

Kit answered, "Me? *Ow!*"

8

Even though her pet did not seem enthusiastic, Tilly started at once to design a space ship big enough for two travelers. She decided to name it the *Zoom Broom*.

To build the *Zoom Broom* she would need material much
stronger than metal, and much lighter. She began to stir
up a new kind of brew in her big iron caldron.

Into the boiling pot she threw some copper coils, a pair of suspenders, a wad of tinfoil, three pounds of beeswax, six containers of "silly putty"—and, for good luck, she added one ladybug wing.

Tilly stirred and stirred, all the while chanting charms and spells. And at last, to her amazement, she found that she had concocted a material as fantastic as plastic!

12

She poured it into a mold she had hollowed out of an old dinosaur's tooth.

When she had made all the parts for the *Zoom Broom* she glued them together with extra-strong, fast-hardening glue.

Then she propped up her space ship into launching position and filled the tank with enough jet-black magic to send them to the moon—and even higher.

She zipped herself into a space suit she had stitched
together out of inner tubes from spare tires.

16

And now came Tilly's biggest problem: how to coax Kit to
stay in the cockpit. "Let mee-out! Let mee-out!" he yowled.

But the minute she said they would probably be flying through the Milky Way, Kit settled down without another yowling word.

Now they were ready to blast off. Tilly Ipswitch, Space Witch, strapped herself into the pilot's seat and began the countdown.

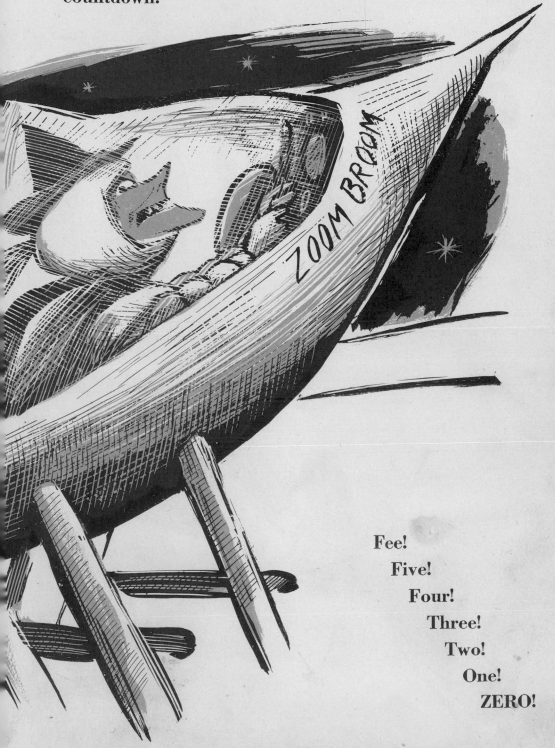

Fee!
Five!
Four!
Three!
Two!
One!
ZERO!

Up whooshed the *Zoom Broom,* high into the sky!

Hour after hour Tilly and Kit swerved and curved, sailing farther and farther away from the earth.

At noon the following day they zoomed over the moon.
But they couldn't see a single creature to scare—only dry,
empty craters, and tall spearlike mountain peaks. So off
they streaked in search of the planet Mars.

But the *Zoom Broom*, with a will of its own, turned and headed for the planet Saturn instead. Tilly shook her head as they came close. "No siree!" she said. "That can't be Mars —not with that burning hoop whirling around its middle. Oh fiddlesticks, we're way off our course!"

On and on they cruised, looking for a place to come down. But they couldn't land even on Jupiter because of the mist. Tilly was disgusted. "Fee-fi-ho-hum, all this flying around and we haven't found a single creature to scare!"

Kit didn't make a sound. All he wanted was to find solid ground and something to drink.

Suddenly Tilly shouted, "Look up there! The Milky Way straight ahead!"

But not a single drop of milk did they see in all that field of twinkling stars.

And even a cat could tell they were lost.

All at once the *Zoom Broom* began to sputter and zigzag very queerly. "Toads and adders!" Tilly wailed. "We're running out of jet-black magic!"

They were streaking wildly toward a spinning planet when—*zoing!*—the space ship slipped down between two sharp mountain peaks and screeched to a stop.

Tilly peered out of the cockpit and exclaimed gleefully, "Kit, we've made it! We've landed on Mars. Now we surely can find somebody to scare."

They scrambled out into the eerie moonlight and as Tilly started to climb down the steep cliff she caught sight of a swarm of tiny lights bobbing around on the level ground below. Outlandish-looking creatures with large heads and very small feet could be seen trotting back and forth and making weird, hornlike sounds.

"Why, Kit, those creatures must be Martians on the march!" cried Tilly. "What a grand treat we'll have frightening them off their silly little feet!" The creatures, however, had spied the earth visitors and vanished in a twinkling!

Kit could think of nothing but finding something to drink. He headed straight for a strange, lonesome-looking house and darted through an open door.

Tilly dashed after him into a dark empty room. And—bang!—the door slammed shut behind them. "Come out, my pet," Tilly urged. "These Martians might not like an earth cat snooping around in here."

At that very instant there came a sharp knock at the door!

"Now's our chance," whispered Tilly and made the scariest face any witch had ever made. Kit bristled his fur and bared his teeth, prepared to spring at anything alive!

Slowly, slowly, Tilly opened the creaky door, and just as she was about to leap out there came a terrific shout.

"TRICK OR TREAT! TRICK OR TREAT!" screamed a flock of flapping little ghosts—the most terrifying band of Halloweeners any witch had ever seen!

Poor Tilly, she was swept completely off her feet, and down she fell in a dead faint. As for Kit, no rocket ever zoomed past faster!

The playful children gathered around Tilly, thinking she was somebody dressed up like a silly old witch. "We didn't mean to scare you so much," said a little girl with a devil's mask on her head. "But you shouldn't have hid in our haunted house."

38

Tilly blinked her eyes and asked, "Wh-who are you? And wh-where am I? And wh-what day is this, anyway?"

"Oh, we're spooks from Pikes Peak, U.S.A., Planet Earth. And it's Halloween!" the children all answered proudly. "Do you want to go spooking with us?"

39

"What did you say? It's still Halloween?" screamed Tilly. Up she jumped and whistled for Kit. "Children, it's time my cat and I were on our way! But first you must fetch me a broom, and then please see if you can find some sour milk for my thirsty kitten here."

Two girls dressed as ghosts ran and fetched a battered old broom, while a boy dressed as a Man from Mars trotted off and found some cream that had just begun to curdle.

Kit had never tasted anything quite so delicious. It suited his disposition to perfection!

The minute Tilly had the broom in her hand she felt like her old self again. She couldn't wait a second longer, and, leaping astride the stick, she mumbled some mystic words. "Mumbo jumbo! Gloom and doom! Abracadabra! Whisk-broom bah!" And off she floated.

As the children watched her glide gracefully up into the sky above their heads they called, "You forgot your cat! You forgot your cat!"

Down Tilly swooped, and as Kit leaped aboard she waved back and said, "Don't worry, I wouldn't forget my pet for worlds. But thank you, spooks, just the same!"

44

Over the rooftops and over the cornfields they flew, homeward bound at last! The witching hour of midnight had not yet struck when Tilly and Kit landed on their own craggy mountain peak.

As soon as she had parked the broom in the broomport
Tilly hurried indoors, slipped out of her space suit and
into a comfortable old calico kimono.

Then she lighted a fire in the fireplace and sat down to pop corn. "Somehow I don't feel quite up to flying around frightening children any more tonight," said Tilly Ipswitch as she yawned a deep yawn. "How about you, Kit?"

But Kit was already curled up in his basket, purring happily in his sleep.